STORIES
for the
Very Young

SELECTED BY SALLY GRINDLEY
• *ILLUSTRATED BY TONI GOFFE* •

Kingfisher

KINGFISHER
An imprint of Larousse plc
Elsley House, 24-30 Great Titchfield Street
London W1P 7AD

First published by Kingfisher 1995
2 4 6 8 10 9 7 5 3 1
This selection copyright © Sally Grindley 1992
Illustrations copyright © Larousse plc 1995

Things That Go Bump in the Day © Tony Ross 1989
Sam Plays the Trumpet © Gabriel Alington 1989
Too Big © Sarah Hayes 1989
The Little Elephant's Next Best Thing © Mary Rayner 1989
The Small Boy and the Lonely Place © John Maguire 1989
The Birthday Gift © Sally Grindley 1989

Material in this edition was previously
published by Kingfisher Books in 1989 and 1992
in *Stories for the Very Young.*

A CIP catalogue record for this book
is available from the British Library

ISBN 1 85697 341 7

Designed by Tony Potter
Printed in Hong Kong

For permission to reproduce copyright material,
acknowledgement and thanks are due to Peters, Fraser &
Dunlop Ltd on the author's behalf for "The Magpie's Nest" by
Michael Rosen from *Story Chest* published by Viking Kestrel.

Contents

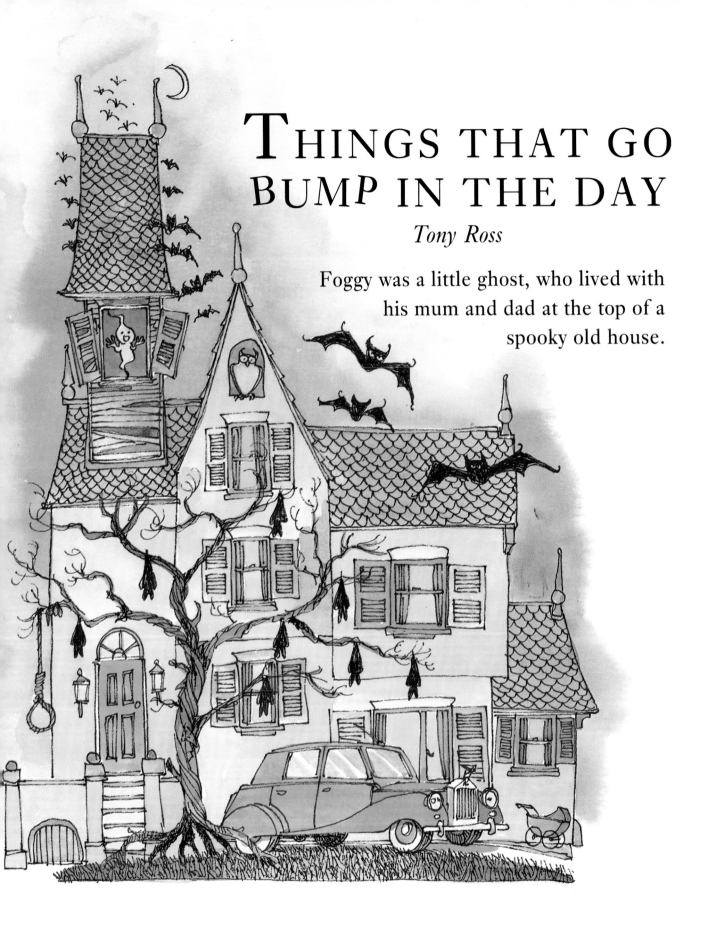

THINGS THAT GO BUMP IN THE DAY

Tony Ross

Foggy was a little ghost, who lived with his mum and dad at the top of a spooky old house.

Foggy was only born about five hundred years ago, so he was a very young ghost. He had lived in lots of places, including a castle, but this was the best. Ghost families like spooky old places because they make them feel safe. This one had lots of bats and spiders for pets. There were woodlice too, but they make rotten pets. You can't teach them anything, and they are not very playful. Foggy nearly taught a woodlouse to sit up and beg, but it kept falling on its back and kicking its legs in the air.

Foggy loved being a ghost. But sometimes life got a little BORING. There are not many things a ghost can do. Then Foggy found a book of ghost stories and things began to get better. The first story was about a ghost who walked through walls. "That'll be a FAB thing to do!" said

Foggy to a creepy slug. And he walked BONK into a wall. All he did though, was bump his nose.

"Shouldn't believe everything you read," giggled the creepy slug.

The next story was about a ghost who walked all over a house shouting 'OOOOOHHH!' and waving his hands in the air, and jumping out of dark places. Foggy thought that was a silly way to behave, but he couldn't get the story out of his mind. There was a whole house beyond the dusty rooms where Foggy lived. Maybe wandering around that going 'OOOOOHHH!' would be less boring than teaching woodlice to sit up and beg.

That morning, when it was time to go to sleep, Foggy's mum gave him a cobweb sandwich and a glass of slime. Then she tucked him into bed.

"Mum," said Foggy, "what's it like in the rest of the house? Are there any dark places?"

Mum kissed Foggy on the bump at the end of his nose.

"Don't you dare go into the rest of the house," she warned. "The rest of the house is a TERRIBLE place. Your dad went there once, and said it was really scary. He said it was horribly CLEAN, and smelt of SOAP, with sunlight all over the place and lots of knobs on everything. UGH!" she shuddered.

Foggy curled up, and pretended to go to sleep. The rest of the house sounded exciting, just like an adventure in a book.

When he was sure his mum and dad were asleep, Foggy got up. He went to the door and, making himself very small, he slithered through the keyhole into the rest of the house.

Foggy floated at the top of some stairs. It was true what mum had said. The house was horribly light, with a funny smell. "That must be soap," shivered Foggy.

Slowly, he went down the stairs. He hovered in the air a little, because there was tickly furry stuff spread all over the floor. He looked around for a friendly bat, even a woodlouse, but there weren't any. "Even the creepies daren't come into this awful place," he said to himself.

With bated breath, the little ghost floated along the

landing. His heart pounded inside him, and he was FAR too frightened to go 'OOOOOHHH!' Foggy wasn't a particularly brave ghost, and by now he was getting really scared. The rest of the house wasn't a good place.

Foggy turned to go back the way he'd come. Then he saw it! If he'd had a skin, he'd have jumped right out of it. It was HORRIBLE.

It was very big, and it was lumbering along clutching a small model of itself. It had blue eyes, with hairs all round them, and matted yellow hair hung in twists down its back. Worst of all, when it opened its mouth to snarl, it showed fearsome white fangs. And it smelt of SOAP.

Foggy reeled. Back along the landing he fled, waving his arms in the air, and shouting 'OOOOOOHHHH!' Up the stairs, through the keyhole, to where his mum and dad sat up in bed, wakened by all the commotion.

"Mum," shouted Foggy. "I'VE SEEN A LITTLE GIRL!"

"Don't be silly," said Mum, cuddling her son. "There's no such thing as little girls."

SAM PLAYS THE TRUMPET

Gabriel Alington

Every day Sam asked the same question.

"Are we going to the park today?"

The park was his favourite place, because right in the middle was a big round bandstand where each afternoon the Brass Band played. Sam sat on the grass in front of all the chairs and listened to the music. It was fine music, loud and exciting. The bandsmen and bandswomen wore red jackets and smart peaked caps. Some of them played trumpets and their bright shiny instruments gleamed in the sun. Sam's mother sat beside him with his small sister, Rosie, till Rosie got bored and had to be taken to see the ducks. Sam never got bored listening to the band. He was going to be a bandsman when he grew up.

"I'll play the trumpet," he said, "and I'll wear a red jacket like the people in the band."

On his fifth birthday, his mother and father gave him a trumpet. It was bright and shiny like the trumpets in the band. Sam took a deep breath and blew into the end, but no sound came out. He tried again, puffing out his cheeks. Still nothing happened. Then his father had a turn. He blew and he blew and his face went very pink, but the trumpet would not make a single toot.

"It needs a lot of practice," Sam's father said. "You'll have to keep at it."

Sam did keep at it. He took the trumpet to the park and blew it all the time the band was playing. But no toot came out. Then one day, towards the end of the concert when the music rose to a mighty peak, there was a moment's pause. The conductor waited with both arms raised, the whole audience held their breath – except for Sam. He went on blowing. And suddenly, to his great surprise, the trumpet gave a TOOT, loud and shrill. TOOT, TOOT, TOOT, it went.

Everyone round him turned and stared.

"Shush," they all said. "Shush. Be quiet."

Sam blushed and stared at his shoes, but he could not help smiling. He had TOOTED his trumpet! He wished his mother would come back from the duck pond so that he could tell her.

When the concert was over, one of the trumpet players in the band beckoned to Sam.

"Me?" said Sam, pointing to his chest.

The Bandsman nodded and beckoned again, so Sam took his trumpet and climbed the steps onto the bandstand.

"That's a pretty nice instrument you've got there," the Bandsman said.

Sam held out his trumpet. "You can blow it if you like."

"We'll swap," said the Bandsman, handing Sam his.

It was big and very heavy and when Sam blew into it no noise came out. Then the Bandsman tried Sam's. Nothing happened. He tried again – and again.

"It's a bit difficult," Sam said.

"You show me then," said the Bandsman, giving the trumpet back to Sam. So Sam showed him. TOOT, TOOT, TOOT.

"That's splendid," said the Bandsman. "You'll be a fine trumpeter one day."

He turned and called the rest of the band. "Hey, come and hear this." The others gathered around Sam while he played for them. TOOT, TOOT, TOOT.

When Sam's mother and Rosie came back from the duck pond, they were surprised to see him on the bandstand. Sam waved to them and played an extra loud TOOT. His mother laughed and clapped her hands. Rosie clapped too. And then all the bandsmen and bandswomen clapped as well. Sam blushed again and stared at his shoes.

He felt he would burst with happiness.

THE
MAGPIE'S NEST

Michael Rosen

Once a long time ago, when winter was nearly over and spring had nearly begun, all the birds were busy starting to build their nests. There they all were: the robin and the eagle, the seagull, the blackbird, the duck, the owl and the humming-bird, all busy. All, that is, except Magpie. And she didn't feel much like working.

It was a nice day and she was out and about looking for scrips and scraps and bibs and bobs for her collection of old junk – her hoard of bits and pieces she had picked up from behind chimneys or from drain-pipes. Pebbles, beads, buttons and the like, anything bright and interesting or unusual, Magpie was sure to collect. Just as she was flying along on the look-out for a new treasure, she caught sight of Sparrow, her mouth full of bits of straw and twigs.

"What are you doing, what are you doing?" said Magpie.

"Building my nest," said Sparrow, "like you'll have to soon." "Oh yes?" said Magpie.

"Yes," said Sparrow, "put that milk-bottle-top down and come over here and watch. First you have to find a twig, and then another twig, another twig, another twig, another twig . . ."

"Don't make me laugh," said Magpie, "I know, I know, I know all that," and off she flew. And as she flew on looking for scrips and scraps and bibs and bobs she came up to Duck who was upside down with her mouth full of mud.

"What are you doing, what are you doing?" said Magpie.

"Building my nest," said Duck, "like you'll have to soon."

"Oh yes?" said Magpie.

"Yes," said Duck, "throw away that old earwig and watch me. After you've got all your twigs you have to stick them with mud pats like this – pat-pat, pat-pat, pat-pat . . ."

"Don't make me laugh," said Magpie, "I know, I know, I know all that," and off she flew. And as she flew on looking for scrips and scraps and bibs and bobs she saw Pigeon with a mouthful of feathers.

"What are you doing, what are you doing?" said Magpie.

"Building my nest," said Pigeon, "like you'll have to soon."

"Oh yes?" said Magpie.

"Yes," said Pigeon, "put that bus ticket down and come over here and learn how. You have to make yourself warm and cosy – right? Right. So you dig your beak into your chest like this – right? And find one of those very soft fluffy feathers down there and you lay that out very carefully inside your nest to keep it warm and cosy, warm and cosy, warm and cosy . . ."

"Don't make me laugh," said Magpie, "I know, I know, I know, I know all that," and off she flew.

Well, not long after that it was time for Magpie to lay her eggs and she looked out from her perch and saw all the other birds sitting in their well-built, warm, cosy nests, laying their eggs. "Oh no," said Magpie, "I haven't got anywhere to lay mine! I'd better hurry." And she remembered Sparrow saying something about twigs, and Duck about patting them and Pigeon saying something about cosy feathers. So she rushed out and quickly grabbed as many twigs as she could, made a great pile of them, threw a feather on the top – and the milk-bottle-top and the earwig and the bus ticket and she *just* had time to sit herself down and lay her eggs.

And if you look at a magpie's nest you'll see it's always a mess. And she ends up throwing her scrips and scraps and bibs and bobs in it too.

I think she likes it like that.

TOO BIG

Sarah Hayes

There was once a giant who lived in a house on top of a hill. At the bottom of the hill stood a little town. The people in the town were afraid of the giant. They called him 'Too Big'.

But Too Big was a gentle sort of giant with a very soft heart. And he was lonely. He wanted to be friends with the people from the town. Once he even invited them to dinner.

"We can't possibly go," said the mayor. "He's far too big. His giant's feet would squash us all. And how would we sit down on his enormous chairs? After all, he is the biggest giant in the world."

Then the mayor wrote Too Big a letter saying that everyone was too busy to come to dinner. After that, the giant stayed in his house on the hill and never came out.

Sometimes children came to play on the slopes below the giant's house, and one day a little girl climbed right up to his front door and began to bounce her ball against it. Too Big heard the knocking of the ball and hurried to open the huge door. When they saw the giant, the children screamed and ran away. All except one, and that was the little girl with the ball, whose name was Elspeth. When she saw the giant, Elspeth took a step back.

"Hm," she said, "you *are* big."

"Yes," said the giant sadly. "Too big."

"Nonsense!" said Elspeth. "Can I come in?"

Then Too Big told Elspeth all about the invitation he had sent. "The mayor said everyone was too busy to come," said the giant.

"Nonsense!" said Elspeth again. "They're just chicken!" Then she had an idea.

A week later an enormous striped tent appeared outside the town. It was the biggest tent in the world. A long line of people waited patiently at the entrance. And inside the tent Elspeth and Too Big the giant began to serve out the biggest ice creams in the world.

When the mayor saw the biggest ice creams in the world, he marched up to the tent.

CLICK- A-TA   CLICK-A-TA   CLICK-A-TA   CLICK-A-TA

"Those ice creams are too big!" he shouted. "They'll make you sick!"

"Nonsense!" shouted everyone else, and for once the mayor had nothing to say.

All summer long Too Big and Elspeth served ice creams, and the giant was happy. But when winter came, it was too cold for ice cream. The giant had to take down his tent and go home. Biting winds swept through the huge house on the hill. Too Big shivered with cold and misery. None of his friends from the town ever came to visit him now, not even Elspeth.

The fact is that Elspeth was far too busy to visit the giant. And so, for that matter, was everyone else in the town. If Too Big had climbed down the hill and listened at the locks and keyholes, he would have heard a mysterious clicking noise coming from every house in the town, even from the mayor's. CLICK-A-TA, CLICK-A-TA, CLICK-A-TA went the noise. But Too Big didn't climb down the hill, and he didn't hear the mysterious CLICK-A-TA, CLICK-A-TA, CLICK-A-TA noise. He just stayed indoors and felt miserable.

Then, one morning, Too Big heard someone knocking on his front door. No one was there, but on his doorstep lay an enormous parcel. Slowly the giant undid the wrappings. Slowly he lifted the present out and held it over his head. Then he pushed his arms into the armholes, and pulled his present down over his head. Over his chest it went, over his tummy, and right down . . . over . . . his knees. It was the biggest sweater in the world, and it was . . . too big!

"Oh no!" said Elspeth, who had been hiding behind a rock.

"It's too big," said the mayor, who had been hiding too.

"Far too big," said everyone else from a hundred different hiding places.

"Nonsense!" said the giant. "It's perfect!"

And when everyone woke up in the cold of the next morning, they found the biggest caravan in the world parked outside the town. Inside the caravan sat the giant in the biggest sweater in the world. And he was serving out the biggest baked potatoes in the world. And no one, not even the mayor, said the words 'too big' ever again.

THE LITTLE ELEPHANT'S NEXT BEST THING

Mary Rayner

There was once a little elephant who lived in the hills of South India, with his mother and all his aunties in the teak forest.

One day, he was splashing about in the river while his mother was being bathed. He squirted water at the other young elephants, and they squealed and squirted back. Then the little elephant looked up and saw a balloon floating high in the sky. And underneath the balloon was a basket, and in the basket, just looking at the view, was a man. I should like to do that, thought the little elephant. It would be better than splashing, better than squirting. It would be the next best thing to flying.

He asked his mother how he could go up in a balloon.

"Don't be silly," said his mother. "You are too small."

So the little elephant waited for the weeks to go by, and then he asked one of the aunties.

"Don't be silly," said the aunty. "You are too heavy."

Oh dear, thought the little elephant. First I was too small and now I'm too heavy. I shall eat less, and *then* I will be able to go up in a balloon.

So he stopped crunching up bamboo leaves, and every time he was hungry he thought about floating through the sky, until the man who looked after the elephants said:

"Dear me, this little elephant is getting too thin. Little elephant, what is the matter?"

The little elephant said, "I want to be thin because then I will not be too heavy to go up in a balloon."

"Ay yai," said the man. "But little elephant, you are *growing*, you will soon be too big."

The little elephant began to cry.

"It is not too late," said the man kindly. "We will get a balloon made. Soon, soon. All we need is money." So he thought and he thought, and then he said, "Little elephant, come with me, and we shall go to the town."

They waved goodbye to the little elephant's mother and all the aunties, and set off together for the big town. They walked along the hot dusty road for miles and miles, past fields of sugar-cane and groves of coconut palms and across a dry river bed.

"I am thirsty," said the little elephant.

"Soon, soon, we shall be there," said the man.

They came to a stall beside the road, next to a garage. The elephant man asked for a cup of tea, and a drink for

24

his elephant. The elephant filled his trunk with water from a bucket, squirted the water into his mouth and drank it all down. The man fetched some more.

Just then a bus drew up, full of people. The driver got out and said, "I need more petrol, and no one can see out of the windows because they are so dusty."

The little elephant became very excited. "I will squirt the windows clean," he said.

"Tell all your passengers to give money," said the elephant man, "and my elephant will clean your bus."

So the little elephant squirted water all over the bus, and all the passengers were pleased, and gave baksheesh to the elephant man.

When the bus had gone the garage man said, "That

was good. If you would like to stay in the compound behind my stall and garage, you can clean all the buses which stop here. Everyone likes your elephant."

So the elephant man and the little elephant stayed for many weeks, until they had cleaned a great many buses and saved up a great deal of money.

"Now it is time to go to the town," said the elephant man. They waved goodbye to the garage man and set off again along the hot dusty road to the town. They went to find the man who made hot air balloons.

The elephant man explained that the little elephant wanted to ride in a balloon.

The balloon-maker shook his head. "That is not possible," he said. "Your elephant is too heavy."

"Can you not make me one specially?" asked the elephant man.

"Not possible," said the balloon-maker.

"We can pay," said the elephant man, and he tipped out fat bundles of rupees in a heap on the ground.

"Perhaps possible after all," said the balloon-maker. "Come back in three weeks."

The little elephant and his friend went away, and they waited for three weeks, and then they came back again.

The balloon-maker had made a beautiful orange and yellow balloon. It lay on the ground behind his shop and tied onto it was an enormous basket, an elephant-sized basket with some extra space for the elephant man.

"Now I will tell you how to do it," said the balloon-maker, and he showed them how to fill the balloon with hot air to make it rise up into the sky.

So the balloon was filled with hot air, and just as it lifted off the ground the little elephant and his friend scrambled into the basket. Up into the sky they went, and they waved goodbye to the balloon-maker. Slowly all the white houses of the town and even the big palace became tiny, tinier than toys. They floated along above the dusty road, over the dry river bed and over the coconut palms and over the sugar-cane fields until they came towards the hills.

On their way they saw the garage and the stall, and they waved, and the garage man waved back and cheered and clapped. And they passed a bus full of tourists, and they waved, and the bus driver and all the tourists waved back and cheered and clapped.

It was just getting to be evening when at last they came to the teak forest. Now they could see the river. They came down a little lower, and the little elephant began to squeal and trumpet, because he could see his mother and all the aunties being bathed.

All the big old elephants looked up, and they saw the great orange and yellow balloon, and the little elephant waving his trunk, and his friend beside him.

"Just look at my son!" said his mother, and she put up her trunk and trumpeted to him.

The balloon came down on the ground, and the little elephant climbed out. His mother and all the aunties welcomed him back, and all the young elephants had an extra splashy and squirty game with him because he had been away for so long.

THE SMALL BOY AND THE LONELY PLACE

John Maguire

One day, in quite a big room in quite a big house, the different places were talking. They were all saying how important and special they were.

"Oh dear, I'm so tired!" said the Place Just Inside The Door. "Everyone walks on me when they come into the room. Then they walk on me again when they go out. I sometimes feel quite exhausted. Still, that's only to be expected –

I'm *quite* the most important place of all."

"Oh yeah, says who?" said the Place In Front Of The Fire. "They mostly come to me. I have the big couch and the armchairs. In the winter I have a lovely hot fire to keep them warm. In the summer I have a beautiful bowl of flowers for

them to admire. *I* am where they spend most of their time, all through the year."

Then the Place In Front Of The Window said:

"What about me? I don't need any old flowers. In the summer you can see the whole garden through my big window. Even in the winter you can see all the world outside. Sometimes people stand here, just looking out, for ages. *I* am beautiful *and* important."

"But where would anyone be without me?" asked the Place Under The Shelves. "If anybody wants to put on the stereo, or get down a book, or talk on the telephone, they have to come to

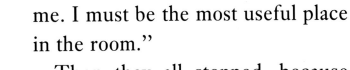

me. I must be the most useful place in the room."

Then they all stopped, because they heard a very quiet sound. It was one you would hardly notice.

"Excuse me," said the little dark Place Behind The Armchairs. "I

31

just wish I was important or beautiful or useful or something. I think you're *all* very lucky."

"How *dare* you even talk to us!" said the Place Just Inside The Door. "What are you, anyway, only a silly dark corner behind the armchairs? Nobody ever goes into or out of you!"

"Yes, indeed," said the Place In Front Of The Fire. "Nobody ever sits down in you to have a nice time. They probably don't even know you're there!"

"Nobody ever sees anything nice or interesting from you!" said the Place In Front Of The Window. "You really aren't an important place at all."

"Look, you haven't even got a carpet!" said the Place Under The Shelves. "All you do is gather dust."

The little dark Place Behind The Armchairs didn't say anything more. It was very lonely and wished that it had *something* to feel important, or beautiful, or useful about. It just wasn't fair.

The next day was *awful*. It was cold and rainy. The clouds were very low, and everywhere was gloomy. All the places in the room were dark and dreary, and nothing nice was happening.

Outside the room there were angry voices in the hall. Mum and Dad and all the children were cranky. Nobody knew what they wanted to do, and nobody wanted to do what anyone else wanted either.

Then the door of the room opened quite quietly. A

small boy came in. He was the youngest of the family, and he was having a terrible day. Everyone was cross; everyone was fed up; everyone said 'No!' even before he was able to ask them anything. Nobody wanted to play with him, and he kept getting in everybody's way.

So the small boy had come into the room. He wanted some quiet time on his own. He knew the way that awful days like this went. His parents had told him to go away, but in a few minutes they would be looking for him crossly. They'd want him to tidy his room or put away his pencils or help with the washing-up or something. He was going to keep out of their way and have a good quiet time all to himself.

He stood just inside the door for a minute. Then he went over and stood by the shelves. Then he stood in front of the fireplace. Then he went over and looked out of the window. But he didn't feel better in any of these places. He looked around, and suddenly he noticed something new – there was a very secret, dark little cornery place behind the big armchairs.

He went straight over and wriggled in there. It was a small place, but then he was a small boy and that suited him very well. It was a very quiet place, but that was just right because he wanted a very quiet time.

"I think this is a *great* new place," said the boy out loud. "It's just what I wanted. It's nice and small and quiet, and nobody has to come here to do things, so I can hide here whenever I want to. It hasn't even got a carpet, so if I drop biscuit crumbs or spill lemonade, I can wipe it up and no one will ever know."

"This place is going to be my special hideaway. It'll be my secret cubby-hole. It's just great."

All the other places could hear the small boy talking, and for once they were lost for words. The small boy and the lonely place were going to get on fine.

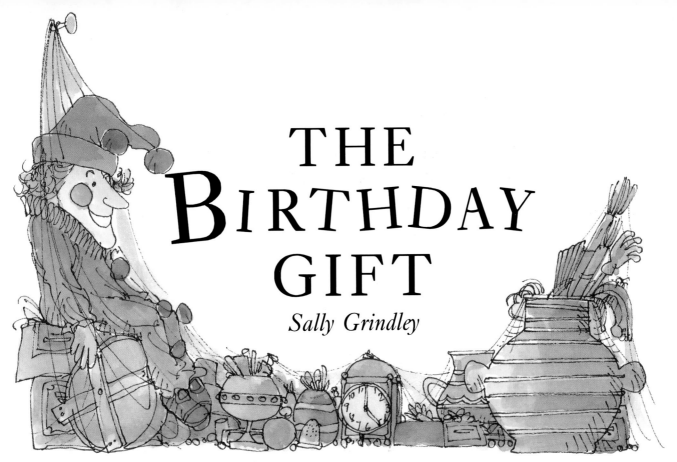

THE BIRTHDAY GIFT

Sally Grindley

On the corner of a narrow street lost on the edge of town stood a little junk shop. Its long unwashed windows were all flaky paint and cobwebs and you could barely see in. If you pressed your nose hard against the glass, you could see shelves crammed with a higgledy-piggledy assortment of pots and pans and vases and candlesticks and books and pictures and oh so many things that you didn't know where to look. Most of them were dust-gatherers and had been there forever. But hanging in the corner was a beautiful string puppet of a clown. One of its strings was broken, but otherwise it was just like new and its smile beamed out through the dirt all around.

Amy and her father often passed the shop but never bothered to look in. Then one day Amy stopped and pressed her nose up against the filthy window. When she

saw the puppet, she jumped up and down excitedly and
called her father over.

"Look at the clown," she said. "Oh Dad, can I have
him? Please can I have him?"

"We'll see," said her father. "It's your birthday soon."

Amy wanted and wanted and wanted the clown. Every
time they walked near the shop, she rushed up to the
window to make sure he was still there.

"How long is it till my birthday?" she asked her father.

"Four weeks," said her father.

"Is that long?" she said.

"Not long," he replied.

Two weeks later, she asked the same question.

"How long is it till my birthday now?"

"Two weeks," said her father.

"Is that long?" she asked.

"Not long," he replied.

Some days later, she asked again.

"Tomorrow," said her father. "It's your birthday tomorrow. We'll go out together to buy your present."

"The clown?" begged Amy.

"If that's what you'd like," said her father.

Amy could hardly sleep that night, she was so excited. And she was restless all morning, until at last her father said that the shops would be open and he was ready to go. She skipped along beside him, chattering away about the clown and how pleased the clown would be to leave the filthy window, and how she would make him dance, and how she would hang him by her bed at night, and how the string needed mending and he would do it, Daddy, wouldn't he? and how her friends would all want to play with him.

At last they reached the junk shop. When they opened the cracked wooden door, a bell rang and an old man appeared behind the counter.

"Can I help you, sir?" he asked.

"Yes," said Amy's father. "I'd like to buy the clown puppet you have hanging in the window. It's my daughter's birthday and she's set her heart on it."

"Many happy returns to you, my dear," said the man. "I'll just go and fetch him. He's a beautiful piece of work, the best in my shop."

While the man was busy taking the puppet out of the window, a woman came into the shop. She stood by the counter and waited impatiently to be served. The man reappeared and went behind the counter with Amy's clown. He laid it down while he searched for some wrapping paper. When the woman saw the puppet she let out a cry.

"Wait," she said, "you're not selling that, are you?"

"Why, yes, madam," said the man. "This gentleman is buying it for his daughter's birthday."

"But he can't!" cried the woman. "I must have it. Billy's set his heart on it."

"I'm sorry, madam, but this gentleman was here first."

"I know," said the woman, in despair. "It's just that my son is very ill in hospital and I promised him the puppet for his birthday. His birthday's not for another four weeks, but I thought if I bought the puppet now it would cheer him up. He's been going on about it for ages, you see."

The man stood in silence and looked at Amy's father. Amy's father looked at Amy. Amy looked down at her clown. With a big effort she said very quietly:

"He can have the clown."

The woman rushed over to her and thanked her over and over again.

"You're a good girl," she said, with tears in her eyes. "I'll tell my Billy what you did for him."

Amy's father picked her up and hugged her.

"We hope Billy gets well soon," he said to the woman.

Amy chose a pair of roller skates instead for her birthday, and it was not too long before she forgot her disappointment over the puppet clown. Then, a few weeks later, she was shopping in town with her father when they saw the woman again. She waved excitedly and ran over to them.

"You're the little girl who gave up the puppet clown for my Billy. I'm glad I bumped into you. Billy's better. He was in hospital for six weeks but now he's better. And he loves that clown. He takes it with him everywhere, makes it dance, even hangs it up by his bed at night. Would you like to come to tea one day and meet Billy?"

Later that week, Amy went to tea with Billy. He showed her the puppet clown, still smiling and with the string mended. Then his mother gave her a box wrapped in 'thank you' paper. Amy opened it very carefully, lifted up the cross of wood, disentangled the strings and pulled gently, and out of the box danced – a puppet lion! A shaggy-headed, swishy-tailed, loppy-legged lion with a great big smile. Amy shrieked with joy.

"He's beautiful," she said. "He's so beautiful."

Billy danced his clown over to Amy's lion and they performed the first of many wild and happy jigs together.